T0206569

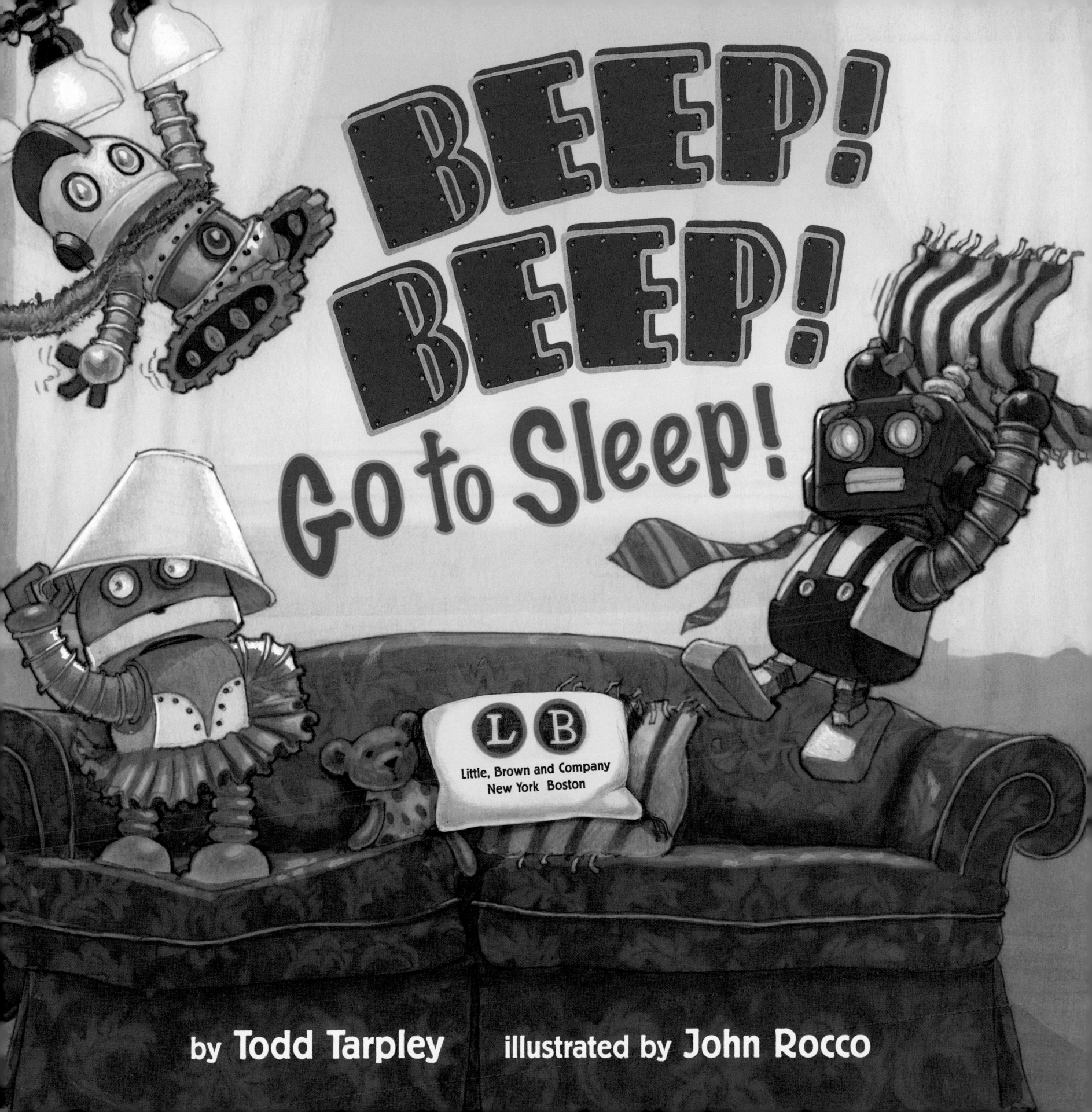

by Todd Tarpley illustrated by John Rocco

Three little robots, time for bed.

Time to dim your infrared.

Brush your rotors 'round and 'round.

Clean your shields . . .

. . . and power down.

Quiet at last, not a peep.

Three little robots are . . .

BEEP!
BEEP!
BEEP!

Is something wrong?
I need my coil!

My sensor aches!
I want more oil!

Better now? Then rest your head.

Three little robots back to bed.

Quiet at last, not a peep.

Three little robots are . . .

BEEP!
BEEP!

What is it now?
I need a light!

My fan belt's loose!
My bolt's too tight!

Quiet at last, not a peep.

Three little robots are . . .

BEEP! BEEP!
Robots!
Are you still awake?
Engines off,
for goodness' sake!
No more beeping!
No more talking!
No more squeaking!
No more squawking!
No more blipping!
Blinking-boinking!
Winking-whirring!
Squinking-oinking!

Oinking?
GO TO SLEEP!

Quiet at last, not a peep.

Three little robots are . . .

BEEP! BEEP!
WHAT NOW???

You need what?

Oh, a bedtime story.
3 LITTLE ROBOTS

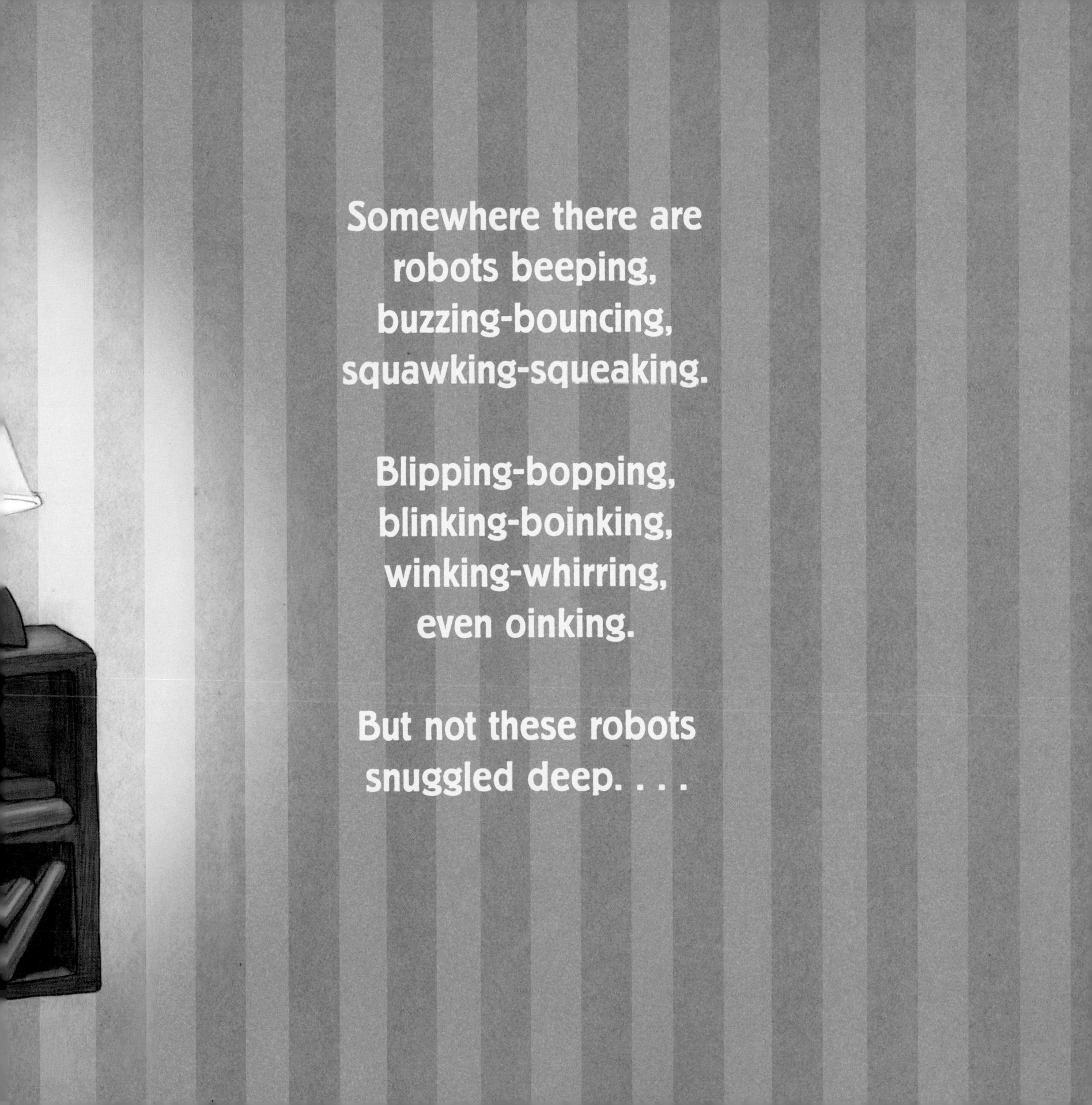

Somewhere there are
robots beeping,
buzzing-bouncing,
squawking-squeaking.

Blipping-bopping,
blinking-boinking,
winking-whirring,
even oinking.

But not these robots
snuggled deep. . . .

They've finally put
their boy to sleep.

The art for this book was created with pencil, watercolor, and digital paint. The mouse was my daughter's idea.
—John Rocco

The text was set in Berliner Grotesk, and the display type was hand-lettered. This book was edited by Liza Baker and Allison Moore and designed by Saho Fujii. The production was supervised by Erika Schwartz, and the production editor was Wendy Dopkin.

Text copyright © 2015 by Todd Tarpley • Illustrations copyright © 2015 by John Rocco • Cover art © 2015 by John Rocco • Cover design by Saho Fujii • Cover © 2015 Hachette Book Group, Inc. • All rights reserved. In accordance with the U.S. Copyright Act of 1976, the scanning, uploading, and electronic sharing of any part of this book without the permission of the publisher is unlawful piracy and theft of the author's intellectual property. If you would like to use material from the book (other than for review purposes), prior written permission must be obtained by contacting the publisher at permissions@hbgusa.com. Thank you for your support of the author's rights. • Little, Brown and Company • Hachette Book Group • 1290 Avenue of the Americas, New York, NY 10104 • Visit us at lb-kids.com • Little, Brown and Company is a division of Hachette Book Group, Inc. • The Little, Brown name and logo are trademarks of Hachette Book Group, Inc. • The publisher is not responsible for websites (or their content) that are not owned by the publisher. • First Edition: September 2015 • Library of Congress Cataloging-in-Publication Data • Tarpley, Todd. • Beep, beep, go to sleep / by Todd Tarpley ; illustrated by John Rocco. — First edition. • pages cm • ISBN 978-0-316-25443-4 (hardcover) • [1. Stories in rhyme. 2. Bedtime—Fiction. 3. Robots—Fiction. 4. Toys—Fiction.] I. Title. • PZ8.3.T1476Be 2014 • [E]—dc23 • 2013023723 • 10 9 8 7 6 5 4 • APS
PRINTED IN CHINA